Bon Appétit, Bertie!

JOAN KNIGHT
WITH ILLUSTRATIONS BY PENNY DANN

DORLING KINDERSLEY
LONDON • NEW YORK • STUTTGART

A DORLING KINDERSLEY BOOK

First American Edition, 1993   2 4 6 8 10 9 7 5 3 1

Published in the United States by
Dorling Kindersley, Inc., 232 Madison Avenue, New York, New York 10016

Text copyright © 1993 Joan Knight
Illustrations © 1993 Penny Dann

Library of Congress Cataloging-in-Publication Data

Knight, Joan.
    Bon appétit, Bertie! / by Joan Knight; illustrated by Penny Dann - 1st American ed.
    p. cm.
    Summary: Something interesting and special happens to the Bonfigs when they visit Paris
with their son Bertie.
    ISBN 1-56458-195-0
    [1. Paris (France) -- Fiction.] 1. Dann, Penny, ill.
    II. Title.
    PZ7.K738Bo   1993
    [E] -- dc20   92-54319
                                                  CIP
                                                     AC

Printed in Belgium by Proost.

The Bonfig family never went anywhere or did anything special. Mr. and Mrs. Bonfig sometimes wondered whether something interesting would ever happen to them, but it never had. Still, Bertie Bonfig remained hopeful.

That was why they were all surprised one day to receive a letter telling them that they had won a free trip to Paris, France. There were three plane tickets and a map of Paris with the letter.
"That's very strange, there is no return address, but never mind, let's go," said Mr. Bonfig.
"A trip?" said Mrs. Bonfig, over and over again.
"When do we leave?" asked Bertie, tucking the map into his pocket.

A few days later a chauffeur-driven car arrived and took the Bonfigs to the airport. After a long flight they were in Paris, zooming down a boulevard in a French car.

"There's the Arc de Triomphe!" Bertie exclaimed.

"Oh, là là!" said the driver. "Tell me, how do you know this?"

"I have my map," said Bertie.

6

Sacré Coeur

Centre Pompidou

Montmartre

Palais
du
Louvre

Notre-Dame

Île de
la Cité

Place de la
Bastille

Musée
de Cluny

Île
Saint-Louis

7

"And there's the Eiffel Tower!"
cried Bertie.
"Can we go up to the top?"
he asked his parents,
but they had fallen asleep.

Mr. and Mrs. Bonfig woke up when
the car screeched to a stop.
"Voilà!" said the driver. "Votre hôtel!"
"It's our hotel," Bertie told his parents,
and out they climbed.

"Bonjour!" said the porter. He picked up their bags and led them into the entrance hall. "Bonfig - Room 22," the receptionist told the porter.

Once they were settled in their room, the
Bonfigs felt hungry. They hoped someone would
bring them something to eat. But no one came, so
Mr. and Mrs. Bonfig dozed off to sleep again.

Just then, Bertie heard someone walking down the hall.
"If I follow him, maybe I'll find something to eat," he thought.

So Bertie followed the man down the hall . . .
into the elevator . . .

and through the cellars until they came
to the kitchen.

LA CUISINE

18

Bertie had never seen such a busy kitchen, or smelled such wonderful smells. He marched up to the chef with the tallest hat.

"Could we have some dinner, please?" he asked.

The chef looked puzzled.

Then Bertie remembered his room number.

"Dinner for 22, please," he said.

"Ah, for twenty-two . . . vingt-deux personnes!" said the chef, handing Bertie a menu.

"That will take some time."

Bertie couldn't read the menu because it was in French, so he pointed to what he wanted.

Menu

poulet

Soupe à l'oignon

Pommes frites

mousse au chocolat

tarte à la cerise

fromage

glace

Meanwhile, in Room 22, Mr. and Mrs. Bonfig had woken up to find that Bertie was nowhere in sight. Mr. Bonfig called the receptionist . . .

while Mrs. Bonfig ran to the window.
"Bertie! My Bertie!" she wailed.
"Where are you, Bertie?"

The receptionist called
the hotel detectives,

the hotel detectives called the gendarmes,

the gendarmes called the chambermaids,

the chambermaids called the porters,

and some passers-by turned up, too.

1 un 2 deux 3 trois 4 quatre 5 cinq 6 six 7 sept 8 huit 9 neuf 10 dix 11 onze 12 douze

Finally, along came Bertie with the dinner.

13 treize 14 quatorze 15 quinze 16 seize 17 dix-sept 18 dix-huit 19 dix-neuf 20 vingt 21 vingt-et-un 22 vingt-deux

And a good thing, too, because everyone had begun to feel very hungry.

Bon Appétit!

melon

poulet rôti

Poisson

Pain

Crème

sucre

mousse du chocolat

tasse

café

Petits pois

fromage

verre

tarte à la cerise

beurre

assiette

Pâté

thé

jus d'orange

Vin blanc

vin rouge

pain grillé

soucoupe

sel

poivre

glace à la fraise

fraise

Pommes frites

Pomme

Pêche

baguette

cuillère

Soupe à l'oignon

fourchette

Couteau

bol

31

The Bonfigs never did find out where those tickets to
Paris came from, but they're awfully glad they went.
They're still enjoying their adventures and each other.
Even the goldfish sees things differently now.